# Faith Of A Child
## *The Genesis*

Sophia Yolanda

Entegrity Choice Publishing
PO Box 453
Powder Springs, GA 30127
info@entegritypublishing.com
www.entegritypublishing.com

Printed in the United States of America

The views expressed in this work are solely those of
the authorand do not necessarily reflect the views of
the publisher, and thepublisher hereby disclaims any
responsibility for them.

The publisher is not responsible for websites (or their
content) that are not owned by the publisher.

Library of Congress Cataloging-in-Publication Data
ISBN:  978-0-692-90991-1
Library of Congress Control Number:  201895299

# Contents

## Part I

## Part II

# Part III

# Part IV

# Part V

Part V

# Part I

# School Girl Reflections –
# A Romance Begins

*"Therefore I say unto you,
'What things soever ye desire,
when ye pray, believe that ye receive them,
and ye shall have them.'"*

### *Mark 11:24 (KJV)*

Mark 11:24 was the first scripture I ever meditated on and received in faith. Standing on it, I received my first answered prayer. Through it, I began a lifelong journey; a romance that would last forever.

I was eight years old when I first received the message of the Gospel: salvation through the shed blood of Jesus Christ. My childhood was already hard by the standards of some, yet easy by the standards of others. As then the only child of my parents, I was often a loner when it came to being at home or even around my many cousins. My mom would say it afforded me the opportunity to get everything I wanted. However, around my extended family, the story was different. They were all light skinned African Americans, with pronounced Native American features. However, I was told often I was "black like my daddy." So, I chose to be by myself rather than suffer the constant ridicule and rejection of the closest members of my family. There were one or two cousins I clung to, but for the most part, I chose to be by myself than be with them. To me, it made the difference to not be simply "tolerated" by people. Even so, my hardships of alienation and isolation didn't end there.

Ever since I can remember, I witnessed the constant abuse and battery of my mother. Before I go there, know this--I love my daddy with all my heart and praise God today he at least strives to serve Christ. However, during my formative years, he was abusive toward my mommy, both physically and mentally. The abuse was never directed at me personally, but I lived in constant fear for her. I would brace myself every night he came home, not knowing what kind of night it would be. I didn't know whether they would be calm and civil to each other or if I'd soon hear the loud cussing and fist blows. I vividly recall times when he'd beat her with the buckle of a belt and I was asked to clean and pour alcohol on the lashes on her back, scars which are still there today. Over the course of time, I watched the soul of this vibrant, beautiful, athletic young woman deteriorate into one who is broken, sickly, depressed, and wheel chair bound. It was as if I witnessed the murder of my mother's soul. Being only a child, I felt powerless to rescue her.

As a result of the rejection, ridicule, and the intensely violent atmosphere in which I lived, I became an angry, yet fearful and bitter young girl. Many would look at me during those times and just say I was a "mean little girl." I lashed out at others in school, starting fights and even rumors so I could see others fight. In terms of being fearful, I avoided others completely. Visitors would come to our house and I would run to my room so they wouldn't see me. I just didn't want to deal with people. I had no clue whether they would be accepting of me or reject me like my family. So, avoidance felt like my best option. I would go so far as to pull stuffed animals out of a toy chest in a closet and hide there, pulling the stuffed animals back on top of me just to avoid interacting with them. During those years, my way of preventing ridicule and rejection was to stay away from people altogether. Overall, I was heading in the wrong direction early in life.

In the midst of all that, I heard the message of Jesus' love. What I received that day was pure love, acceptance, and grace. I embraced Christ and with that, His awesome Word. It was an Easter Sunday morning when I received the Gospel of Jesus Christ. My Aunt Gloria had taken me to church because she wanted "a little girl she could dress up." With tears streaming down my face, during the invitation, I asked her if I could go up to the altar and she responded yes. She knew my dad, being a Muslim, wouldn't approve. I'm so glad now she was bold enough to do what she felt was right. So, at the age of eight, I was saved while belonging to one parent who was an alcoholic and another who was an abusive, practicing Muslim. You can probably guess my salvation wasn't celebrated as much as it would be in your typical Christian household; my family considered me to be "doing my thing."

Soon after that experience, I heard a TV preacher preach from Mark 11:24. I couldn't go to church or read a Bible in my home because my dad, being a part of the Nation of Islam, would not allow that "white man's Bible" in the house. However, the TV was in my room and no one monitored what I watched on TV.

So, this TV preacher preached Mark 11:24 and said if you believe that scripture, God will give you what things so ever you desire, "point your hands to the screen." I did and I asked God for the thing I desired most: a little brother or a little sister.

I was so excited after that prayer, I ran in the room where my parents were and told them what I asked God for. My dad laughed and said, "How do you expect God to do that without us?"

I didn't have an answer to his question, but I believed Mark 11:24. That next year, my sisters—yes, twins--were born! Glory be to God! After that first answered prayer, no one could make me believe God wasn't real and He didn't love me. I knew God was real and more importantly, I knew He loved and accepted me. Thus, the romance began.

This first section includes poems and inspirations I received reflecting upon these early years. God showed Himself strong on my behalf. I went from getting bad grades in school to being an honor roll student. I went from having few friends to being able to move confidently in and out of various circles in school. Even when I wanted to play outside, I recall praying Elijah's prayer to stop rain and God honoring even that. I would play in the wet grass and when I was done, go inside and watch it start raining again. God truly honored my faith during those younger years! Through signs, miracles, and wonders worked in my own life, He cemented my faith in Him, this Faith of a Child. My faith ultimately became so strong that once the trials of adult life hit me, people wondered at my stability, faith, and maturity in God.

There are some who say if you get children involved in faith too early in life, they will resent you and not stay in the faith. That clearly was not my experience. I don't know where my life would have been if God did not invade my reality when He did. For that, I am forever grateful. Long live my God and King and I pray all little children everywhere, whether their lives are easy or hard, come to know the friend who is our Lord and Savior Jesus Christ. Hallelujah! Let all the earth praise the Lord. Praise the Lord! As you read these next pages, I pray you will be blessed.

# Faith of a Child

I came to Jesus while yet a child, but
    innocence was already lost.
Daily witnessing my father's rage, my
    mother's own holocaust!
Anger and terror gripped my soul as I felt
    hopeless and alone,
But then I met Jesus, with love and grace and
    all my rage was gone!

Surviving in darkness, time moving on, the
    only child my parents knew,
Skin dry and darkened, features full and
    flawed, un-favored whispers I drew!
Then the God of heaven touched my eyes, to
    that fearfully and wonderfully made,
And all the darkness disappeared and my past
    began to fade!

As grace took root, faith became its fruit,
    along with joy, peace, and love!

Prayers were uttered, declarations made, and
    heaven's windows opened from above!
God smiled on me and answered my prayer
    for a young sister or a brother.
It didn't matter to me, but to Him you see,
    twin sisters were made to order!

I loved them so much, gave them all I could,
    while yet still a child,
But age doesn't matter with the Father and
    faith and grace to make one smile.
One answered prayer led to another and so
    our relationship grew,
This was Christ's plan, to hold me in His hand,
    always faithful and true!

The Faith of a Child is innocent and pure,
    untainted with worldly views,
The Faith of a Child is trusting and sure, and
    quite easy to subdue.
The Faith of a Child grows and grows, one
    level building upon another.
The Faith of a Child, in the Lord Jesus Christ,
    will endure, forever to prosper!

# Early To Praise
*(written as a song)*

Ear-ly, Ear-ly, Early will I come to praise You.
Ear-ly, Ear-ly, Early will I come to praise
 Your name.

I love you Jesus, these words are true.
I love the warmth, 'tween me and You!

I love the care, You give to me.
I adore the sacrifice that made me free.
I love the words, spoken tenderly.
I honor the works, done faithfully.

Ear-ly, Ear-ly, Early will I come to praise You.
Ear-ly, Ear-ly, Early will I come to praise
 Your name.

Thank you Lord, for never leaving me alone.
Thank you Lord, for helping me push on.
So many times, I wanted to quit.
I said let me dear Lord, just enter my rest.

But, You said to me, no my child not just yet.
I got a job to do, and you're the best.

Ear-ly, Ear-ly, Early will I come to praise You.
Ear-ly, Ear-ly, Early will I come to praise Your
    name!

# Believers' His-tory

Listen and hear a true story to be told,
About the one and only Savior, the faithful
   One of old.
The One who came to set the captives free,
The One who bled and died for you and me.

See way back when the world was empty and
   void,
Our Father sat down to converse with our
   Lord.
He said with a voice forceful and deep,
"It is now time to create the world to be,
Let us form mankind with mind, soul, and
   heart."
So with great anticipation creation did start.

But something went wrong with God's
   companion and friend.
Mankind was not faithful till the very end.
He allowed rebellion and sin to reign.
He jumped aboard Satan's wickedness train.

When God looked down and saw what did
   come,
His heart filled with sadness and gloom
   dropped like a bomb!
Suddenly He decided within Himself,
"I'll raise up a holy nation to serve Me and no
   one else!"
The nation He did raise and showed them His
   wonders and powers.
He led them and protected them every minute
   of the hour.
All the people around them wondered at the
   miracles they could see,
And questioned among themselves just who
   their God could be.

But even with that the people did turn.
Obedience and love God's heart did yearn.
"The people," He said, "are filthy with sin.
Soon my only choice will be to let destruction
   come in."
But the Word, the Son, knew of the Father's
   dilemma.
He knew that somehow as for mankind, He
   must save them.

He said, "I know what they need, a payment
    for sin.
Once they are free, their hearts I will win."
"I'll show them the perfect way to live and
    serve the Father,
Then to love one another won't really be much
    harder."

So then was born Jesus, our Savior and Lord,
He set us free from sin so heaven's train we
    may board.
Now we may live in peace and with much joy
Because of that perfect gift, that glorious baby
    Boy!

And this my friends is why our children must
    know
Of the true, true story that happened long ago.
The schoolbooks are great, and so is college,
But our children will perish, if they lack this
    knowledge!

# If It Had Not Been For the Lord on My Side

If it had not been for the Lord on my side, now
let the Christian say,
If it had not been for the Lord on my side, I
would not be here today!
If it had not been for the Lord on my side,
when troubles came my way,
If it had not been for the Lord on my side,
dragons and serpents I could not slay!

If it had not been for the Lord on my side, to
chase my fears away,
If it had not been for the Lord on my side, the
wages of my sins I'd pay!
If it had not been for the Lord on my side, His
word I could not obey,
If it had not been for the Lord on my side,
from the road to eternal life I'd stray!

If it had not been for the Lord on my side, now
  let the Christian say,
If it had not been for the Lord on my side, God
  only knows where I'd be today!

# God Is Watching

*(written as a song)*

God is watching you!
He's got His eye on you!
He's got His angels writing all that you think,
     feel, and do!

Why do the heathen rage?
And, imagine wicked deeds?
The Word of God is what we all must one day
     learn to heed!

God is watching you!
He's got His eye on you!
He's got His angels writing all that you think,
     feel, and do!

He hears the words you say,
And, even the thoughts you think!
You better set your heart on Christ or your
     ship, it will sink!

God is watching you!
He's got His eye on you!
He's got His angels writing all that you think,
    feel, and do!

So many people doing -
All sorts of evil things!
They just don't know the kind of judgment it
    one day will bring!

God is watching you!
He's got His eye on you!
He's got His angels writing all that you think,
    feel, and do!

Oh nations hear us calling!
We're crying out to you!
We want to see you saved, for we know the
    Lord will see you through!

Don't you feel Him watching?
Staring through the sky?
Get your life in order now, or you will truly die!

God is watching you!

# Reflections of Paradise
*(Paradise Missionary Baptist Church,*
*Atlanta, GA)*
## My Home Church

Reflections of the Paradise I've grown to know
Hasn't really changed from what it was long ago.
The sweet smiles from some of our mothers
    you see,
Are still the same way they used to be.

Sis. Alva White, full of wisdom and grace,
And even Sis. Little with a Spirit-filled smile
    on her face.
Mother Price with expressions of kindness in
    her eyes,
And Sis. Spear with the deep, cool voice, none
    despise.

The legendary Mother Drummer, mothers
    everyone with care,
And our own Sis. Thomas, who's always
    willing to share.

On the door is Ms. Moore always ready to
Praise the Lord,
And her beautiful sister, both of which I truly
adore.

Our dear Deacon Pullen, with a constant
extended hand,
And even Deacon Hathaway, with the tender
nod and grin.
Deacon Canty, everyone knows he's been
changed,
And quiet Deacon Grant, whose peace will
always be the same.
I know our church has had its ups and downs,
But with all our trials and tribulations, we're
known to turn around.
Paradise to me will keep getting stronger and
stronger,
Our destiny is sure to last much longer.

When you look real close, we haven't changed
from long ago,
For the true, sincere love will always be in the
Paradise I know!

*Given: October 22, 1993, Church Anniversary*
*Written by: Sophia Yolanda Malcolm*

# The Way It Was Meant to Be – Accepted!

Father God in heaven, holy is Your name. Lord, I love You dearly and Your word is my constant inspiration, confirming for me the things You speak to my heart. Lord, Your word sings to me of Your love, grace, and mercy. I am sometimes bewildered by those three. Oh Lord, give me understanding!

Thus says the Lord, "My child my love for you is deep and intense. I long to receive your sweet praises."

O Lord, the child in me longs to be in Your presence at all times, under the shadow of Your wings; a place secret from the world and its evil. Out there Lord is nothing good for me. They laugh in my face because You made me the way I am. I'm pierced with their arrows of rejection.

Thus says the Lord my God, "Never have I created a thing and replied it was not good. You are my creation, if I have accepted you, who then can reject you? You were created for My good pleasure, please Me! I am your Father and your God and there is no rejection in Me! Consider now, have I rejected you? Do I not call you My child? What is the world that it should put down one I have raised up? Look to Me, I am He who perfects those things that concern you. You have no reason to fear the rejection in their faces or the scorn from their mouths. My love is perfect and it casts out all fear! If there were a part of you that was not meant to be, then that thing about you would be changed. My child let not the world mold your love for me. Don't be convinced by their lies and blindness. Let them not hinder you from the things I have called you to do!"

# Sweet Memories

Sweet memories of my faithful God and
    Friend
Will abide with me till the bittersweet end.
No longer fretful of the things to be,
No longer doubtful of what should happen to
    me!

I remember the times of deliverance and
    power.
I remember the timely salvation of the hour,
With kindness and tender mercies so deep,
With love and grace I should forever keep.

See God has proven Himself wise and true.
He's shown me in trials He'll see me through!
Although sometimes doubt tried to reign,
I knew that faith in God should remain.

I'm so happy with this God I've come to know
Even in my pain, affliction, and woe.
I've never been deserted in my time of need!

I've always gotten the victory; I'm forever to
    succeed!

Remember the goodness God has done for
    you!
Remember all the hard times He's brought you
    through!
Don't let the enemy kill your trust in your
    Friend!
For our God is indeed faithful to the end!

# Part II

# College Life – Time to Grow

*"He that observeth the wind shall not sow;
and he that regardeth the clouds shall not
reap. As thou knowest not what is the way
of the spirit, nor how the bones do grow
in the womb of her that is with child:
even so thou knowest not the works of God
who maketh all. In the morning sow thy seed,
and in the evening withhold not thine hand:
for thou knowest not whether shall prosper,
either this or that, or whether they both
shall be alike good."*

**Ecclesiastes 11:4-6 (KJV)**

I was at Tulane University in New Orleans, LA. Those times were like a roller coaster to me as I'm sure college years are for many. Coming from a predominately African-American environment where family, friends, and every professional I encountered in my life looked like me, I was instantly thrust into a racial mixture more aligned to the "real world." I saw there both the good and bad of the various races. I was met with much discrimination that up to that point had only been a part of black history month, never my reality. My experiences at Tulane made the plight of the "Negro in America" real to me.

Unfortunately, in spite of the good people I met (I still love my first roommate), I began to grow bitter and angry toward other races. I started understanding my father's hatred of Caucasians at that point and began to empathize more with him. However, God would not allow me to settle in hatred and that mindset. I had to grow spiritually and here's how God "grew me up."

After Rita, I had gone through several roommates that were nothing like her. These people were evil and did unthinkable things to me. I requested a different room and finally ended up by myself. One night I had a dream. That dream is explained in an inspiration you'll read called "Day of Visitation".

That day was indeed a Day of Visitation and it scared me so much that to this day, I don't judge things as I see them, while they are in a temporary state. Nothing is permanent for me. God has power to change any situation in a matter of time and is especially skilled at making all situations work together for my good.

One time in particular was during my final semester of senior year at Tulane. I was coming from Christmas vacation and my mom had spent her last to get me from Atlanta to New Orleans. When I got there, I realized there was a long line to register. People were being turned away because of finances. I went to the finance office first because I knew my circumstances. There was another long line and when I entered the office, I saw one student rush out crying because they wouldn't give her a waiver to register. I thought to myself, Wow they're being strict if even the Caucasian students are leaving in tears. Then came my turn and the person I met with appeared to be one of the leaders in the office. He looked at my account and said, "You owe quite a bit. Do you have money to pay?"

What I owed was in the thousands. I responded no and he asked, "Can your parents get a loan?"

I again responded, "No, they've taken as many loans as is allowed." He asked, "Can they mortgage the house?"

I said, "We don't own our house."

He asked, "Can they get a pawn on the car?"

I responded, "We don't own our car."

He looked at me and looked at my account. He looked again at me and looked again at my account. Finally he said, "Well, I don't have the heart to stop you! Here, go register!" I took my waiver and got to the register's office as fast as my legs could take me.

I grew quickly during this time and learned to trust God even more. This next set of poems and inspirations speak most to this time. Enjoy and continue your own growth in God. Be blessed!

# Day of Visitation

The cares of the world had surrounded my mind. My thoughts were clouded by the memories of everything that had ever happened that was of bad report. Imaginations of what could go wrong followed them. My love for God and for man had passed lukewarm and was on its way to being cold. Peace had packed her bags and joy was running close behind. Even sleep decided it no longer wanted any part of me. In my mind, the world was my enemy and my God was just sitting by.

Then one night when I caught hold to sleep, a dream interrupted my rest. I was on a beach at night, sitting upon a huge rock. As the waves of the sea roared, a voice began to say to me, "He who observes the wind shall not sow, and he who regards the clouds shall not reap. As you do not know the way of the wind, or how the bones grow in the womb of her who is with child, so you do not know the works of God who makes everything."

In my foolish wisdom, I replied to the Voice, "I do know how a baby grows. After the egg is fertilized, it begins to divide--" but the Voice cut me off and thundered to me, "You don't know how bones grow in the womb and you don't know the works of God!"

Then I felt someone roughly shake my body, in order to wake me. When I awoke, I found no one there! Later on that day, my Sunday school teacher directed us to Ecclesiastes 11. There were the same words from the dream. I didn't recall ever reading this scripture before, but right then I realized what the words were and Who spoke them. The Lord Himself had to visit me and tell me that I can't view what's going on around me and determine His plans for my life. Whatever He told me to do, I had to do, despite how things appeared on the outside. I had to let Him be God and lead me on! For He is the One who will perfect those things that concern me! He is working His perfect work in us all! Let God be God!

–Tulane, 1988

# Promises, Promises

My Lord, where would I be without Your promises? What would I do if You changed Your mind as easily as the wind changes its direction? Father, what would I do if You decided to no longer care, to leave me in my ways, doing as I please? Lord, where would I go if You no longer held Your loving arms open to me? Who would I run to when I was alone? Who would I talk to when I needed a listening ear and an open heart? Dear God, where would I run when my enemies came against me? Who would I turn to? Lord, I don't play their games. I've never had that desire. I wouldn't know the first move to make against them. Lord, without You I would die. I'd no longer have a reason to live. Lord, without You I would not know how to live. How would I survive in a cold, heartless world I barely understand?

Father, thank you for Your promises. Thank you, O God, for being my faithful Friend. Thank you, Lord, for comforting me. You comforted me even when there was no one to turn to, no one to explain my feelings to, no one to understand my point of view.

Thank you, Father for Your patience, when I did things my way and turned my back on You. Thank you Lord for correcting me when I'm wrong and showing me a better, happier more peaceful way to live. Thank you Lord for loving me anyway! Lord, sometimes I wonder where I would be if You were as critical of me as I am of myself and others, or if You were as impatient with me as I am with others. Thank you, Lord, for being the way You are, full of love, mercy, patience, kindness, peace, and grace! Thank you, dear Father, for being just the way You are!

# The Son Behind the Clouds

The songbird sings, "What shall I do?" No man knows the answer. God alone knows our life's plans. He knows where He will lead us, what we will encounter, and how we will overcome.

Often the clouds of despair get so thick. Lord, how can we see through them? In our minds we know not to fret, yet worries still come. In our hearts we know to trust You, yet that peace seems to fade. Those clouds are all we see. Oftentimes, with clouds comes stormy rain. Many times, you can even smell the rainstorms in the air...

The Lord spoke to me saying, "When those natural clouds are out and you can't see with your physical eyes the sun, yet you know the sun hasn't disappeared, it hasn't left you, nor has it been destroyed. But the sun still shines with all its glory behind the clouds.

"So it is with the trials and tribulations that afflict you. You must remember even when a cloud of despair shadows your vision the Son of God is still shining in all His Glory! He has not forsaken you, nor can He be defeated and destroyed. He will move those clouds and, just as your natural sun, will allow the morning to come again!"

# Pep Talk

Many are the afflictions of the righteous, but the Lord delivers them out of them all. Quiet my soul while the Lord is in His Holy temple. He is working His perfect work within you. Take your rest in the Lord while He leads you gently through your trials, tribulations, and afflictions. Whoever has no rule over his spirit is like a city that is broken down, and without walls *(Proverbs 25:28, NKJV)*. This fiery trial is but to purge you and to produce within the precious fruit of God's Spirit.

Have your hope in the Lord. Take your rest in the knowledge of His faithfulness and love for you. "No weapon formed against you shall prosper" *(Isaiah 54:17, NKJV)*. Satan is fighting another losing battle. His futile attempts will lead to nothing. Call his work as a work of naught. Know in your heart that Jesus is Lord. He reigns with all power and majesty. Blessed be His holy name.

# Let's Talk

Come talk to me, cries our Lord
Knowing I'll see you through
Come talk to me, says my God,
Knowing I died for you

Tell me all about it, God says
You know how I care,
Your heart, thoughts, your very soul
I'm here for you to share.

Why do you keep those burdens
Locked, hidden deep inside?
You know I can see all things,
From Me you cannot hide.

Let Me take good care of you,
In you I wish to reside.
Let Me carry that load for you,
For you I came and died.

I, the Lord, cry out to you,
I hurt when you feel the pain.
For I have been where you are now,
My peace and joy you'll gain.

Cast your cares upon Me,
Tell me all your heart.
For this will lighten the load you bear,
This will give you a fresh new start!

Come talk to Me, cries our God!
Share with me your thoughts,
Come talk to Me, says my God,
By Christ's blood you were bought!

Come and talk to Me, God says
These things true friends do,
Come and talk to Me
On the cross, I've died for you!

Whatever is on your heart
Pour it out to Me,
Tell me all your mind
Soon, you will see.

My dear child, you can always
Come talk to Me!

# Who Am I

Who am I, Lord, that You make Your grace sufficient for me, or Your power perfect for me? Why do You even care about my weaknesses, especially just to make me strong? I am but a small part of this universe You've made. Why have You brought Yourself low to see about my needs? Why do You care about my prayers? Why do You even take time to listen? Your love and passion for even the smallest members of this universe is simply amazing!

What is it You find in me that makes You care so much? Does my praise drive Your passion, though a song bird I am not? Lord, Your passion for me preceded my praise for You! Is it my witness or service? Lord, it's by Your Spirit I can do all things! Why me Lord? Why do You care? Oh Lord, Your love is great, Your mercy is everlasting. I don't understand the depth of Your love for me. You found me when I was a little child. There was little right with me, as a matter of fact, there were a lot of things wrong.

Whatever the reason Lord, I love You too. You knew that would be the case eventually.

That's the reason why!

# What is Man?

O Lord, what is man that You are mindful of him? Also, the son of man, that You visit him? Lord, You have proclaimed to Your servants no weapons formed against us shall prosper, and every tongue that rises against us in judgment, we shall condemn. *(Isaiah 54:17, NKJV).* Lord, what is man that he should receive such promises from the Almighty God?

Father, I praise Your holy name that I have been made in Your image and Your likeness. I praise You Father that You have honored my word and directed my every footstep. O Lord, I sit back and wonder at this mighty shield You have placed around me. You are my fortress and no man or devil can tackle You to get to me.

Dear Lord, Your faithful love and care baffles me. What is man, O God, that You move to save his soul? What is man, Father, that You commission the angels of war at the cry of his voice? Oh, I praise You Father!

For You have said to me that whoever gathers together against me shall fall for my sake *(Isaiah 54:1,5 NKJV)* Again, I ask You Lord, "What is Man?"

# Praise Be To God

*P*raise God! For the Lord will perfect that which concerns me. His mercy endures forever! He will never forsake the works of His own hands! *(Psalm 138:8)*

*Praise God!* Even though my heart devises my way, the Lord is directing every step I take. *(Proverbs 16:9)*

*Praise God!* When I confess my sins, He is faithful and just to forgive me of my sins and cleanse me from all unrighteousness *(1 John 1:9)*. Praise God! As far as the east is from the west has He removed all my transgressions from me. *(Psalm 103:12)*

*Praise The Lord!* For God loves me with an everlasting love. *(Jeremiah 31:3)* His mercy is everlasting, and His truth endures for all time. Thank you Jesus!

*Praise God!* Jesus is the Author and Finisher of my faith *(Hebrews 12:2)*, being that faith is trusting and believing every Word of God, knowing that what is promised is already mine. Praise God! Faith is knowing God loves me so much that He will give me my heart's desire, while the Holy Spirit works in me making God's desire mine.

*Praise The Lord!* Where my faith fails, God's grace begins!

*Thank You Jesus!* Your mighty word brings me comfort, joy, peace, love, and power. Lord, I magnify Your holy name and my soul gives You the highest praise! *Hallelujah!*

# Part III

# Young Adult,
# but Not On My Own

*"When the apostles in Jerusalem heard that Samaria had accepted the word of God, they sent Peter and John to Samaria. When they arrived, they prayed for the new believers there that they might receive the Holy Spirit, because the Holy Spirit had not yet come on any of them; they had simply been baptized in the name of the Lord Jesus. Then Peter and John placed their hands on them, and they received the Holy Spirit."*

### Acts 8:14-17 (NIV)

It was scriptures like the one above that ushered me into my young adult years. I'd read them and prayed to God saying, "Why hasn't anyone laid hands on me to receive the Holy Spirit?"

Since the age of eight, I had only been baptized with water baptism. Baptism in the Holy

Spirit, with the evidence of speaking in other tongues, wasn't taught in the traditional Baptist church. (The concept of "full gospel" Baptist church wasn't yet a part of my reality in the early 1990s). Each time I read scriptures about the signs, miracles, healings, and deliverance ministered through spirit-filled people, I thought and prayed to God that I was missing out on "more of Him."

I even remember praying one time to God, "The world would be a much better place, with more people getting saved, had You not stopped the baptism of the Holy Spirit." Can you imagine that? I was counseling God!

During this same time, my cousin told me about a church that practiced the laying on of hands and prayed speaking in tongues. I told her it was scriptural, but I'd never heard of a church doing those things. So in summer 1991, she invited me to visit her church, The Sword of the Lord Ministries with Bro. Randy Hall, Prophet. What a Prophet he is! This man was truly anointed with Word of wisdom (foretelling the future) and Word of knowledge (knowing intimately an individual's past). When I saw the working of miracles there, I said, "See God, this is what you should have everywhere"! After a few Sundays, I joined that ministry and received for myself the Baptism of the Holy Spirit with the evidence of speaking in other tongues! Since then, I'm constantly amazed at the signs, miracles, and wonders God works in my life and in the lives of others through me. It's truly amazing!

With the Baptism of the Holy Spirit and praying with my spirit (i.e. speaking in tongues), doors began opening in every area of my life. For instance, just out of college, I realized I didn't want the jobs that came with my degree. They felt boring to me. Almost a full year after graduation, I took an entry-level position at Grady Hospital, the public hospital here in Atlanta. Six months after I began working there, only a few months after I received the Baptism of the Holy Spirit, one of my directors approached me with a brand new position being created. He said he prayed about it and God showed him I would be a good fit. (Did you get that? A corporate leader admitted God told him I'd be a good candidate for a job I knew nothing about.)

After getting that promotion, several people, that had been at Grady fifteen years before me filed a grievance with HR at their being over-looked for the job. Of course, treating the Baptism of the Holy Spirit as a "new toy" I prayed for that too. Eventually, HR upheld my promotion! There was no stopping my prayer life from that time forward. Even now, I pray for everything! I don't care about anyone's opinion on it; I trust praying in the Spirit before trusting my prayers in English.

In addition to career growth and economic prosperity, I began laying hands on the sick and watching them recover. I started receiving dreams and visions of people I knew and they were amazed at how accurate my "word of knowledge" was for their lives. Words can't describe the amazing grace I witnessed in my life.

Near the end of my young adult years, I experienced greater spiritual warfare along with the signs, miracles, and wonders. I quickly learned of my family's history with sorcery and witchcraft, encountering both angels and demons. Don't worry, I won't get super-deep on you, but I will say I experienced my greatest highs and my deepest lows. I'll briefly describe what I mean:

At the sword, I met a man who had been ordained as a leader in the church. He told me the Lord told him I should leave my current boyfriend (who had just started talking marriage) and be with him. Because he was an ordained leader in the church and had his own street deliverance ministry, I didn't question him. I left my boyfriend and within one month of dating I became his fiancé. We ministered together. As he preached on the streets, I would pray and prophesy to those who came to our makeshift "altar." People were getting blessed, but after a while I became weary with it. One morning, I took the bus to his house so we could go to church together. When I got there, he said he was too tired to go. We ended up that day falling into sin. I won't go into details about the sin, but know for me it was devastating. I felt God had to now curse me because I had disobeyed His word. I put myself on "ministerial punishment" by not ministering anymore. (This was neither God's word or will but my own foolishness and guilt!) I didn't teach, I didn't lay hands on anyone, and I wouldn't pray for anyone. I felt a "breach" between God and me.

Later, I would be riding the MARTA train and reading my Bible when a stranger sat next to me and asked what I was reading. I read the scripture to him and he asked me what it meant.

I said, "It means that you can't judge a situation before its time and God knew the end result of all things."

He asked me, "Are you sure that's what it means?"

I said, "Yes."

He said something to the effect of "I agree," or "I'll believe that too." As I watched him get off the train, I saw him go through the doors, but not on the outside. I promise you, he walked off the train to nowhere; there wasn't anyone on the other side of the train walking away. I wondered to myself if that could be an angel.

Still considering myself on "ministerial punishment," again I was on a MARTA bus when another stranger sat next to me. He started talking to me about being a "Nubian Princess." He made comments about the Qur'an and I kept quiet. Even though I had read the Qur'an, I had placed myself on "ministerial punishment" and refused to teach anyone anything. After a while, he started making erroneous statements about the Bible and Jesus.

I couldn't resist at that point and said, "Look, say what you want about the Qur'an, but don't sit here and lie on Jesus!"

I then began teaching him what the word actually said and what it meant. When the bus reached my stop, he followed me off the bus. He asked, "What if I want to get saved right now?"

I said fine, ignoring my self-imposed "ministerial punishment" and led him in the sinner's prayer. He took off his beanie and threw his Nubian books in a big city trash bin. He told me his father was a preacher and he misunderstood some things about his church.

He was crying and said, "I think I need to go talk to my dad."

I never saw him again, but that day made me realize ministry is by the grace of God. Since it can't be earned, it can't be taken away as a punishment. I had to keep my heart right through repentance and self-searching, but the ministry of God had to continue.

Once I did that, I perceived a restoration with Christ. As for my fiancé, I prayed about him. Randy called and told me my fiancé was actually still married to a woman in California. Despite being told to be honest with me, he was still being misleading and was therefore no longer a leader in the church. The next day at Grady, I had a meeting with the psych department and saw my fiancé sitting there. I asked him what he was doing there and he said he was preaching.

After looking around and seeing one man slouched over, asleep in a corner, I asked, "Who are you preaching to?" He realized I had caught him in a lie and admitted to being a psych patient! Not only was he still married to another woman, but also he had a drug addiction and had recently relapsed. I thought to myself, God, You can do better than this!

Overall I learned a valuable lesson. The call and gifts of God are without repentance, but you know a tree by its fruit (Romans 11:29 and Matthew 7:16). I thought because a leader could prophesy and lay hands on the sick, they were sent of God. What I should have known was it's the fruit of the Spirit (love, joy, peace, patience, kindness, goodness, faithfulness, gentleness, and self-control) that allows a person to be recognizable as a believer. It was a hard lesson to learn, but I'm glad God brought me through it.

So, after ending that relationship, I began meditating on this next set of poems and inspirations you are about to read. Enjoy and be blessed!

# I want to Know You More

*(written as a song)*

I want to know You more,
More and more each day.

I want to know you more,
Know You in each and every way.

You are my Prince of Peace,
The source of all my good success,
The lover of my soul,
You bring me joy and peaceful rest,

I want to know You more.

# The Breach

What a sad thing it is to feel a breach with the Lord. To feel as if everything worth living for was suddenly taken away. To feel all alone, as if your own self had left you.

My God is my closest friend. He knew me in the womb and as a child, befriended my lonely soul. We walked and talked together often. How I loathe growing up and being pushed into the cares of this world, into the busyness of this human race whose love dims in comparison. They can't even closely counterfeit the love my Father has for me.

I had sinned greatly against my God. How I managed such a grotesque feat my soul can only wonder! All I knew was I was no longer close to my God. I thought the one who once kissed me, now had to turn away from me; it felt like a curse. For He is holy and has magnified His word above all His name. Was I immune to the wages of sin?

I have suffered greatly for my foolishness. I went far away from my Lover. I will return! He will again go into me and we will once again be one. For He said to me, "if you confess your sins unto the Lord, He will forgive you of your sin and cleanse you from all unrighteousness" *(1 John 1:9).* This is a great mystery of my Father, my God, my Lover, and my Friend. This is His grace and His mercy! I will again rejoice!

# Godly Sorrow

Lord, as I look back over my life, there are so many words I wish I could take back, so many actions I wish I could erase out of the recordings of my life. You are constantly affirming I'm covered with the blood of Jesus. You remind me since I've confessed my sins, You have been faithful and just to forgive me of my sins, and even have cleansed me from all unrighteousness *(1 John 1:9)*. You say You have removed my sins from me as far as the east is from the west *(Psalm 103:12)*. You remind me that they were cast into the depths of the sea *(Micah 7:19)*.

Lord, I sincerely thank you for Your forgiveness and mercy. For though my sins be as scarlet, they shall be white as snow, and though they be red as crimson, they shall be as wool *(Isaiah 1:18)*. Father God, in the name of Jesus, I pray Lord that You help me to forgive others and myself as You have forgiven me. Help me Lord to put the past behind me and press forward. I know I am not worthy of the salvation You give but help me to receive Your gift fully and freely. Help me Lord to accept and internalize the perfect love You have for me.

# The Personal Intercessor

Thank you, dear Lord, for standing in the gap. For at my lowest times, no man would come near me. Family and close friends, for whom I would have given my life, fled from me. None came near me, or even offered up a prayer on my behalf. The only prayers offered were against me instead of for me.

You O Lord, the Alpha and Omega, the Beginning and the End, the Ancient of Days, You were my Intercessor and the One who pleaded on my behalf. You stopped the evil plans of those who worked iniquity. You saw to it that I was restored to a rightful place.

God, I love You. You are great and fearful, yet compassionate and full of love. My soul fears You, but my heart loves and longs for You.

Thank you, Lord, for not leaving my side. Thank you, Lord, for not leaving me in bondage to the sins of my youth. Thank you, Lord, for the great deliverance where my soul is now free to do as You will. Thank you Lord that in spite of myself, You still love me to forgive me of my sins, save my soul, cleanse me from all unrighteousness, and even place a mighty calling on my life. Thank you, Lord, that I was not left to myself. Thank you, Lord, for being my God, my Intercessor, and my best friend.

# Prayer of Confirmation

The Spirit of the Lord has rest upon me. The Spirit of wisdom and understanding, the Spirit of counsel and of power, the Spirit of knowledge and of the fear of the Lord has all come upon me. I will delight myself in the fear of the Lord. I will not judge by what I see, nor will I decide by what I hear, but I will humbly give up everything to my Father that is in heaven and my Lord and Savior Jesus Christ *(Isaiah 11:1-5)*.

The Spirit of the Lord is upon me, because He has anointed me to preach the gospel to the poor in spirit; He has sent me to heal the brokenhearted, to preach deliverance to the captives, and recovering of sight to the blind, to set at liberty those that are bruised, to preach the acceptable year of the Lord *(Isaiah 61:1-2)*.

The Spirit of the Lord is upon me to be as drunk with the Holy Ghost as the drunkard is with his wine; speaking to myself in psalms and hymns and spiritual songs, singing and making melody in my heart to the Lord; giving thanks always for all things to God the Father in the name of my Lord Jesus Christ. I will submit myself to others in the fear of God, exercising to the fullest love, joy, peace, longsuffering, gentleness, goodness, faithfulness, meekness, and temperance *(Ephesians 5:18-21; Galatians 5:22-23)*.

The Spirit of the Lord is upon me. It replaced that spirit of fear with the Spirit of power, of love, and of a sound mind. It gave me an everlasting joy in knowing that my name is written in heaven! *(2 Timothy 1:7; Luke 10:20)*

# Spoken to the Heart

My Lord said unto me, "I will never leave you nor forsake you. Even in your deepest and darkest trial, I'll be there. None will be able to separate you from My love, grace, and power. Trust Me and know that I am your God and you shall not be greatly moved."

Now, go forth as I have instructed you. Do all I have commanded you to do. For no weapon formed against you shall prosper and every tongue that rises against you in judgment you shall condemn. This is your heritage as a servant of the Most High God, whose love for you is greater than the heavens are wide. *(Isaiah 54:17)* Walk in my love, peace, and joy. Know ye that the Enemy has no power over you. I am your stronghold, your fortress, and no evil can pass through Me.

"Rejoice, the time is near! Rejoice, the time is at hand! Run your race fiercely and complete the tasks that are at hand! For behold, I come quickly. I will reward all according to their works." *(Matthew 16:27)* "Run on, be ye not afraid! For I will always be with you!" thus saith the Lord.

# With Tearing

Forever Lord will I meditate on the wondrous works You have done in my sight. Your love and mercy shall continually be in my heart and the magnitude of Your grace on my mind. My soul shall always bless Your Holy name. Because of You Lord, I was delivered from the tricks of the enemy. When my eyes were closed so I could not discern between the false and true, Your right hand was upon me watching all I say and do. O Lord, I shall never forget all You've brought me through. Glory be to my good God, who loves me!

# My Lord

Patience Lord, sweet patience Lord, have patience with me Lord while I go through these things. I meditate on Your word, yet it takes a trial to make it sink in, to give me the understanding. I learn it, I write it on my heart, yet it takes me a while to get the full revelation. I pray to have patience with me Lord. Your burdens for the world are many, yet You still have patience for me. You have suffered long with me Lord, through tears and travail. You have waited with joy while I broke through into the fullness of Your truth.

Praises Lord, praises unto You! You, O God, who have suffered long with me. Praises to You O mighty One who hurts when I hurt, laughs when I laugh. Praises to the great and awesome God who cared for me. I am lowly and Thou are high, yet You are with me! You are my comfort and my joy. Your Holy Spirit is my midwife, making me to birth those things that are of You.

Thanks Lord, the highest thanks, for the highest God. My soul longs to do more, but I can't measure up to Your grace. I can't give You enough thanks for Your mercy.

Worthy Lord, You are worthy! You're worthy to receive glory, honor, wisdom, and praise. Your blood has made me whole. I shout with laughter, I cry tears of joy, yet all I can say is thanks!

# Part IV

# Marriage Life – For Better and Worse

*"Many are the afflictions of the righteous: but the Lord delivereth him out of them all. "*

### *Psalm 34:19 (KJV)*

Marriage life has been a roller coaster ride out of this world. God blessed me with the meekest and most humble man I could ever have. The roller coaster ride comes from the many trials and tribulations we've encountered as a couple.

We met through a mutual friend who was accustomed to giving me a ride after church. When the friend's car broke down, he asked Earl, my husband, to begin giving both of us a ride home. One night after service, Earl approached me and asked if I needed that ride. When I got into the car, I asked what happened to our other friend. His response was, "He'll be all right." A month later we were engaged and a year later we were married! The rest is history.

Six months into our marriage, I learned I was pregnant with our first son. We were climbing up and on a natural high from life itself. A month before the delivery, I was ordained as a teacher by the same Bishop who married us, Bishop Wiley Jackson, Jr. of Gospel Tabernacle Cathedral in Atlanta, GA. Still climbing high, I delivered my son on June 1. I thanked God for a healthy son, but I had one question for God--why was there so much pain? I believe in natural childbirth. I didn't want any medications or surgery. The burning and pain of child delivery challenged my faith to believe God for even more.

After the birth of my son, my husband wanted me to quit my job and be a stay at home mom. I prayed about it and God showed me in a dream that if I did, we would suffer financially, even to the point of losing our home. I shared with Earl my dream and he looked at me with all earnestness and said, "Sophia, I want you to stay home." So I did.

Six months after that decision, true to the dream, we were homeless! Not only were we homeless, but also I was pregnant with my second child. I was pregnant, with a newborn, and homeless. There was much to pray about on this downward slope.

A few relatives housed us as best they could, but finally one relative told us of an abandoned house she owned in an economically distressed part of Atlanta. When we got there, we found drug paraphernalia and other indicators that the house wasn't totally abandoned, but was being used for other purposes. We put in a mattress and stayed in one portion of that abandoned home.

Housing wasn't the only issue during this time; we also were low on food. My husband walked up and down a main street in Atlanta looking for food. He finally found a restaurant owner who had compassion on us and began sending her patrons to that abandoned house to bring me breakfast in the morning and lunch at noon. She would prepare dinner for Earl to pick up in the evenings. He paid her what he could at the end of the week. She never charged us what the food was really worth. The Lord showed us His mercy and extreme compassion by putting in our path the right people at the right time. All this was in spite of the warnings we received in the dream. God is awesome.

Our blessings didn't stop with housing and food. Remember, I told you with my first child, my faith was challenged with the burning and pain of delivery. So, during our homelessness, I searched the scriptures trying to find a scriptural foundation to believe God for a painless delivery. I learned pain during delivery resulted from a curse during the garden's fall. However, in the New Testament, I found this:

*"Christ hath redeemed us from the curse of the law, being made a curse for us (for it is written, 'Cursed is every one who hangeth on a tree')."*

### *Galatians 3:13 (KJ21)*

I believed God that I had been redeemed from every curse, including one associated with pain in child bearing. I believed God for a home of our own, food for our family, and a painless delivery. Wouldn't you know it, on May 1, God gave us our answer. My daughter's birth was so pain free, she came with four pushes in my sister's apartment. During her birth, I felt only pressure, no burning or pain. My husband delivered her with guidance from 911.

Furthermore, having two babies and without a home gave us a priority listing to receive housing. We received an apartment of our own. Rent for that apartment was low enough that we were able to keep plenty of food in the house. Somehow, God led me in my purchase of groceries so that we had meat and two vegetables for dinner every night, on a budget of twenty-five dollars a week.

Two years after I stopped working, I returned to work taking another entry-level job. I was at that entry level for nine months. I then received a new job, with a different employer, and my salary returned to the same amount I had when I stopped working. A year later, I had received a bonus along with another promotion. We were once again on an upward slope.

This next set of poems and inspirations blessed me during this time. I pray they will now be a blessing to you.

# Somewhere In Heaven on an Altar

If you're looking for problems and some of my
 woes
I gave them to Jesus a long time ago
I tell you one thing to forever know
They're somewhere in heaven on an altar.

You may not see the storms that blow in my
 life,
Or those precious relationships filled with
 strife,
Though the pain feels like a cut with a knife,
They're somewhere in heaven on an altar.

You can't feel my body when it doesn't feel
 good.
You can't see my tears even when you think
 you should.
I would place it in your brain if I thought I
 could,
They're all somewhere in heaven on an altar!

Take this advice I give to you,
Trust in the Lord, He's faithful and true.
There is nothing better that you can do,
But place it somewhere in heaven on an altar.

# The Reason Why I Praise

*(written as a song)*

You are my Father, and the perfect God for me!
You are my Savior, and my highest majesty!
You are my Faithful Friend, through all eternity!

That's why I give my life to You, and praise
your holy name! (2X)

Oh, oh, Prais-es, to the One and only God.
Prais-es, to my Maker and my Lord.
Lift up Prais-es, with our voices and our hearts!

That's why I give my life to You, and praise
Your holy name!

Peace and love come from the touch of Your
hands.
Joy and power from the anointing of Your breath.
Grace and mercy from the depths of Your heart.

That's why I give my life to You and praise
Your holy name. (2X)

# Revive the Passion

God has made the effort to keep me in His will and on the path of righteousness. I often wonder why such pain and effort was dispensed to keep me on the right track, especially when I see so many who have strayed, or never even entered this way. To me, it's more than love, but it seems to be a certain devotion God has to His own. There have been times I became so angry, I blamed God for my circumstances. Later, I would apologize. Still, there were times I was so hateful to His children. I began to hate others and myself, yet He continued to stay with me, waking me up to how things really were. It's as if He was trying to say, "Sophia, don't be upset; things will change, I promise." As though He had to explain Himself to me, trying to make me understand His actions when He is the Almighty God, worthy to be loved and feared no matter what He allowed or decided to do. God is sovereign.

My passion for God has changed tremendously from that of my youth; however, the blessings and miracles have gotten better and more intense. I wonder, why that is so? Then there's Isaiah 2:2: "I remember the devotion of your youth, how as a bride you loved me and followed me through the desert, through a land not sown."

This verse spoke to Israel and now speaks to me. In response, I say, "Lord, I remember Your faithfulness in my youth, how as a Father you loved me and led me on a desert-like journey, through places I'd never seen before!"

To all God's children, this verse continues to speak! God remembers the devotion, love, and passion we had for Him when we first received His saving grace. The "desert" we follow Him through are the different chapters we have in our lives, along with all of its trials and tribulations. As a "land not sown," everything for us is fresh and new. Because God remembers this, He desires to hold on to that passion. His love for us is strong and faithful. Rejoice in the Lord. A God so great and wonderful loves and cares for us. He patiently waits for the passion to be revived.

# For In the Time of Trouble

*Why fret my soul over those things,*
*which are in the hands of the Lord? Don't*
*you know God is the faithful rewarder of*
*those who diligently seek Him?*
*(Hebrews 11:6)*

Wasn't it He who told you whatsoever things you desire, when you pray and believe, you have received them then you shall have them? *(Mark 11:24)* Why do you waste your energy with the cares of this world? Hush, be quiet, be still, and wait on the Lord. He has never failed you. His love for you is too great; too strong to see you fall! How He delights in your praises. Does the just God deserve to have your praises taken from Him? Does He deserve to feel the pain and turmoil that you put yourself through? How happy He is when He proves the accuser wrong. He laughs in his face and loudly proclaims, "This is my child and he pleases Me." My soul, glorify the Lord, praise His holy name, for He is working His perfect work. He is just giving you another testimony in which to proclaim His marvelous works. For with this testimony, you will exalt Jesus, drawing the sinners of this world! *(John 12:32)*

Rejoice for another victory in which you may proclaim the majesty of the Lord. For when has there been a victory with no war, or a testimony to give without first going through the trial? Magnify the name of the Lord. Prove the lying accuser wrong. Let our Heavenly Father be proud to call you His child! Fret not and count it all joy, for God Almighty is the faithful rewarder of those who diligently seek Him! *(Psalm 37:1; James 1:2; Hebrews 11:6)*

# From The Bottom of the Heart

O Lord my God, how precious You are. Once again You have made me proud to call You my Lord. The gods of man cannot measure up to You, O Lord, God of heaven and earth.

Father, once again You've delivered me from the snares of Satan. My enemies will not rejoice over my sorrows because You have transformed me into a mighty overcomer. Glory to Your holy name!

During this trial, how grievous it was to me, I knew through You I was more than a conqueror. Even better, I acknowledged You in all things, trusting You, and in keeping Your word, Your promise, You directed my paths! *(Proverbs 3:5-6)*

Father, You are a great and mighty King, an awesome and Holy God! I smile when I think on the love You have for me. The moment when we feel far apart, You are close. I laugh and consider the triumphs and victories we share.

Blessed be my God!

# A Tender Cry

My Lord, My God, why must man be so evil? What is it inside of us that make us not care who we hurt? Why is it we must constantly "watch our backs," not being able to trust our neighbor?

Lord, how I wish we could love like You love, and care as You care. Don't people realize we could all make it if we pulled together instead of pulling apart? Lord, am I just a dreamer? No! I know in my heart the day will come when only the pure will live. How I wish we all would be there!

# My Lord, I Know

My Lord, I know You love me!
I know You're faithful and true!
I know You're always beside me,
And in trials You'll see me through.

My Lord, I know Your passion for me is deep
    and strong!
I know the depth of Your compassion toward
    me, even when I'm wrong!
My God, I know Your heart toward me, that it
    is good and true.
I know Your perfect will for me much growth
    and stumbling's few!

Now Lord, You know my deepest thoughts
    and my heart toward man and You.
You know my desire for good fruits in my life
    to produce.
Lead me through the trying times with trials
    and battles great,
I know that eternal life is mine if I just walk
    straight.

# Loving God

I was speaking with the Lord the other day when He said to me, "You shall love the Lord your God with all your heart, with all your soul, with all your mind, and with all your strength" (*Deuteronomy 6:5*).

As He was speaking, I thought to myself, it's so easy to love the Lord, why does this even need to be said? Many love the Lord because He first loved them. It's easy to love the Lord because He laid down His very life for our sakes. It's easy to love the Lord because He loves us with such passion and zeal that it's sometimes hard to understand. Then the Lord heard my thoughts and asked me saying, "Why do you think such thoughts to yourself?

Hear what I have spoken to you. I didn't just say love Me, but I said love Me with all your heart, soul, mind, and strength. This means that I'm to be loved above everything else with all the energy you have, even above your very life. As I have lovingly laid down my life for you, I ask you to lovingly forsake this worldly life for me, obeying my commands and worshipping me as you are really in love with me, in spirit and in truth" *(John 4:23-24).*

Yes my child, many claim to love me, but how many love me above everything else?

This is what I want, this is what I desire.

I am the Lord your God, and the love you have for me must be above everything else.

# Part V

# Middle Aged – No Crisis Here!

*"Commit your works to the Lord, And your thoughts will be established."*

### Proverbs 16:3 (NKJV)

*"Commit your way to the Lord, Trust also in Him, And He shall bring it to pass. He shall bring forth your righteousness as the light, And your justice as the noonday."*

### Psalm 37:5-6 (NKJV)

The scriptures above have been the foundation of all my good success in Christ Jesus! Each time there was a new job, a new effort, a new project, and especially a new ministry, I looked to the scriptures above and stood on them in prayer, expecting God to move on my behalf. Even when it came to raising my kids, I committed to God my work and ways with them, so my thoughts concerning them were established. Life hasn't always been perfect and without its share of trials, but I could see God's guidance and direction every step of the way.

After years of continued growth in my career, there came a time when I experienced what I perceived to be an injustice. After receiving congratulations on various projects I felt as though I began being persecuted on my job. It was all much unexpected and from people with whom I thought I had good relationships. I found out the hard way that their smiles and encouraging words were all a lie and a deception. Some even plotted to destroy my character by saying negative things for performance evaluations and feedback. I began to pray and trust God using the scriptures above, committing my ways to the Lord and trusting Him to bring forth my righteousness as the light. He did so in such a major way.

After many bad things were said about me, I started looking for work at other companies. In the meantime, a Vice President at that present company approached me and asked if I would come to work in his organization. In all fairness, I thought he should be aware of the negative things that were being said about me and what had been recorded in my performance evaluations. To my surprise, he wasn't at all surprised. He took me under his wing and gave me enough professional freedom to make major changes throughout his organization. As a result, the final review I had at that organization came from him.

I wasn't even planning on leaving there until I got a call from a headhunter in December 2004. The headhunter said he found my resume on the internet from where I had published it a year earlier, when I was under attack. He admitted he had actually represented me to a company as if I was already signed on with them and asked if I would do "him a favor" by interviewing. (I know what you're thinking and yes, a total stranger called me up and asked for a favor!) He said, "Even if you don't like them, just please help me by giving the interview."

I did and after one thirty-minute interview, I was hired by the company. They never called me in for a face-to-face interview. To my surprise, they even consented to a salary increase of thirty-five thousand more than what I was currently making. I took the job! Years later,

I asked the guy who interviewed me, Mark Richardson, how was it he hired me without ever interviewing me face to face. In his southern charmed voice he said, "Why that's because I had an unction from the Holy Ghost!" It sent chills up my spine!

My success didn't stop with my career. One morning I woke up and decided I wanted to do something different. I went surfing on the internet for women's activities and found women's professional football, full contact, full pads. Of course, I'd never played any sport before, but the promises of the scriptures above weren't limited to family or job. God said I should commit all my ways and all my thoughts and I did. I played as an offensive tackle, #70, for the Atlanta Xplosions.

In 2006, the year I started, I was the only rookie to make the starting line-up. This was also the year the Atlanta Xplosions won their first IWFL Championship game. God moved tremendously that entire season in guiding me in learning a sport I never understood as well as meeting the extreme physical demands of football. Within the first three months of practice, I lost almost forty pounds. My body transformed in ways I never thought possible. There were times in the huddle during a game I thought I would physically pass out. However, I'd pray and believe in God to strengthen my body and was truly amazed at what my body was able to do. At the end of the season, the entire offensive line was so spectacular; we each individually received trophies for being an O-line Woman of the Year! It was an awesome experience.

Today, God continues to do great things for me. My children are awesome, my husband is still as loving as ever, I have good success on my job, and my church family is truly amazing. I sense God is orchestrating every step I take. My entire life is a symphony; God is its maestro! What an awesome wonder He is! Enjoy this last section of poems and inspirations. Although it's the last chapter of this book, trust and believe, my story is still being written.

Enjoy,

# Beautiful

*(written as a song)*

How beautiful, how wonderful, how special is
your holy name!

I love You! I lift You up! I worship and adore
Your name!

You are worthy Lord, worthy of all the praise!

You are awesome Lord, Perfect in every way!

Lord I praise Your holy name!

(Modulate and repeat till you get enough!)

# Behold God

Look all you saints of the Lord and behold
God's grace!
Look all you saints of the Lord and behold
God's love!
Look all you saints of the Lord and behold
God's mercy!

For Satan will try to make you look at his simple world and take on a spirit of jealously, but I say to you stop, look, and behold God! For how can you become jealous of others if you're too busy looking at the God who alone is worthy of all praise, honor, and glory?

For Satan will try to make you take on a spirit of depression, but I say to you stop, look, and behold God! For who can meditate on what they are lacking if they meditate on the God who gives freely to all!

For Satan will try to make you take on a spirit of disobedience. I say to you stop, look straight ahead at God and behold His awesome work! For the fear of the Lord is the beginning of wisdom! *(Proverbs 1:7)*

Look all you saints of the Lord and behold God's Holy Spirit. For if you keep your mind and heart on Jesus, Satan can't make you fall. I say to you saints of the Lord, behold God! For if you want to see His awesome works, praise Him with a truthful spirit, live the righteous life, love with God's unfailing love, stop!

Behold God!

# Prayer of the Saints

Lord Jesus, I thank you for all the love, joy, mercy, peace, grace, and happiness You give me. Daily You renew my strength. You're constantly reminding me Lord of Your love for me. Your love for me is so great that sometimes it's incomprehensible. Your mercy is given freely and abundantly and for that, I praise You!

O Lord, Your goodness is so great to me. You shower me with Your blessings. I wish Lord I could explain to others Your goodness. I wish I could open up their minds and pour in all the knowledge I have of You, so they too can understand that following Your will is the utmost way to live. Living by and obeying Your commands produces the happiest life. Lord Your works are so great that if I didn't know You it would be hard to believe them myself.

O Lord, I love You so that even when I think I'm not being showered with blessings, I'm able to rest in You. You are still able to give me inner peace and joy. What must I say Lord to convince people they should follow You? How can it be said? Lord please give me the words to say. I want to inspire others to have hope in You. I want to lead others to worship You. I want everyone to know and experience the joy and peace of following You!

# For The Love of God

**P**raise the Lord! For His love for us is great, His love is mighty, His love is magnificent, His love is unconditional, His love is wonderful!

Tell me you children of the living God, you saints in the earth, what can you do for the Lord that would equal His love for you? You sing praises aloud, yet His love is still greater. You worship in spirit and in truth, yet His love is unsurpassed. What will you do for the Lord, for the love that He has for you? Will you proclaim His gospel throughout all the earth? Will you write His holy word onto your hearts? Will you live a life holy and acceptable to Him?

I tell you the truth, though you try to imitate God, your love still doesn't compare. Your mercy is cruelty compared to His. Yet, He loves with the highest love. For God is love.

So I say to you, what shall we do for this our Lord, our God who loves past our understanding, past our comprehension? We shall love

Him, obey Him, worship Him, praise Him, with all our heart, with all our soul, with all our might, with all our mind. For this is pleasing to God. Praise the Lord!

# The Cry of the Church

OLord, our strong God, how wonderful is Your name throughout the earth! Your mercy and compassion endures for a lifetime; it passes from generation to generation. Daily Lord, do we cry unto Your holy name. Rid us Lord of the thorns in our side, the ones that defame Your holy name. Purge us Lord of those who would try to destroy Your works and of our own secret faults that keep us from conquering all. Save us Lord from wicked men who have slid in while we closed our eyes. Deliver us Lord from those who would oppress us and hinder us from the work we must do.

Lord, let Your mercy and truth arise in us! Free us Father from the yokes that bind. Anoint us O God, once again to proclaim Your truth and preach deliverance to all mankind! Father, You said in Your word "upon this Rock I build My church and the gates of hell shall not prevail against it" *(Matthew 16:18)*. Remember O Lord, and lift us up in thy former power and strength. Fill us with Your Holy Spirit that our enemies may be conquered. Make us clean that the body of Your Son may rejoice with a loud noise and the high-sounding cymbals.

Thank you Lord. We know our cries are heard. Thank you Lord. We know You will rise to deliver those who love You and call on Your most holy name.

In Jesus' name we pray, Amen.

# A Touch of Reality

The Lord and I were talking over the terms of the contract that was made concerning me, the covenant of which the people of old spoke. He told me all my sins that were confessed and repented of were taken away. He told me of my inheritance and how I had been adopted as a child of the living God. He informed me of the powers and rights I had through His name. He even told me of the troops I had behind me helping fight this war and how He would be busy as my High Priest before the Father, constantly pleading my case. *(1 John 1:9; Ephesians 1:5; Psalm 91:11; 1 Timothy 2:5)*

As He spoke of all the things He had done as His part of the contract, I began to ponder about my side and the things I had to do. I had to put away my old ways of the flesh and put on new ways of the Spirit. What kind of task was that? Who wants to be given into drunkenness anyway, walking around with no mind or will, in a constant state of depression, feeling sorry for myself and seeking empty happiness? Who wants to put up with sexual lusts that lead to no self-respect, and no type of real love worth holding on to? Who wants to live a life of hatred and backbiting, knowing how others will hate you in the end? The life without love is a lonely and empty one. Who would actually want to go around not being loved or being able to love? *(Colossians 3:1-17)*

The more I considered this contract, the more I realized what a good businessperson I must be. I receive love unconditional and life abundantly in return for being obedient and faithful to the commands for my benefit, and the Lord I love anyway. For this way was a happier, more peaceful and fulfilling way to live. *(Isaiah 1:19)*

Then the Lord heard my thoughts, smiled and said, "It is good for you to enjoy the obedience and love that is required of you. However, there is more that I ask you to do. I commission you to proclaim to others the benefits of this contract, explaining to them the intensity of my love for them and bidding them to come to me. In addition, I have an enemy who is constantly fighting against me and the ones I love, attempting to keep me from the lost souls I sacrificed myself to receive. I empower you to war against him and his wickedness until I am ready to receive those waiting for me unto myself. *(Matthew 28:18-20; Luke 10:18-20)*

I thought about this little twist to our contract and the responsibility that went along with it. Fighting for souls and winning them to Christ is a great and awesome task. Then the Lord reminded me the battle itself was actually His. Through His Spirit I would receive power to win souls to Him. As for fighting for souls, I am His battle-ax, the weapon He will use in this battle. Whenever something needed to be bound and called down, He could use my voice and faith to bind it and cast it down. Whenever a soul needed love and attention, He could use my heart with which to love. Whenever someone needed a touch from the Lord, He could use my hands. Whenever someplace needed a visit from the Lord, He could use my feet to get there. He needed a clean heart to house His Spirit and yield itself to do whatever His Spirit gave direction to do. *(Proverbs 11:30; Jeremiah 51:20; Isaiah 62:6-7)*

Then I considered even more and realized I was still on top. Each battle I fight is already won! What then was the hard part of this contract that kept so many lost souls from signing? The Lord looked on me and said, "Too many, my child, just don't understand the terms."

# MAESTRO

God is in control, passionately He orchestrates
My life, my journey, and yes, for me, a perfect
    blessed fate!
This great symphony which is my life,
    through love He initiates,
A holy dance, a Christian waltz, He sanctions
    destiny's date!

It begins with faith, small but sure, on Him I
    stand and wait,
Daily to study His precious word, on promises
    I meditate!
Gradually faith grows and grows, power and
    love demonstrate,
His holy plan, His faithful hand, to open wide
    heaven's gate!

Faithful lover, friend, and Lord, my holy
    heavenly mate,
In me He lives and guides me through Satan's
    treacherous bait!

Though I stumble and sometimes fall, never
    does He hesitate
To lift me up, reset my path, my purpose He
    reinstates!

I love my God, this divine Maestro, the God
    who orchestrates,
His holy purpose, His precious plans, in me
    He impregnates!
On this journey, purpose I carry, destiny in me
    gestates,
Growing to perfection, full term to deliver
    never, ever too late!

I thank you Lord, for my purpose, my journey,
    my perfect blessed fate,
This holy plan and destiny for me You
    faithfully mediate!
Surely all things are still working together for
    good till I graduate,
To Your front door, You have for me in store,
    those pearly heavenly gates!

Blessed be His holy name!

# About the Author

Sophia Yolanda Malcolm Corker is a proud native Atlantan! A member of the generation known to the world as "Generation X," she is reputed for being able to engage and inspire all generations through the love and grace God has given her. She is a mother of two, Robert Earl Corker, Jr. and Faith Bernell Corker, and the wife of Robert Earl Corker, Sr.

As a born-again believer, Sophia accepted Christ at the tender age of eight. Years of studying the Word of God and walking in "gifts of faith" led her to be ordained as a teacher in May 1997, licensed as a Minister in June 2017. Today, Sophia continues to intercede for the people of God and teach the Word as often as the opportunity presents itself.

The inspirations and poems contained in this short volume were written during the course of Sophia's young adult to middle-aged years. Be blessed and inspired as you journey with her through joy, tears, blessings, and trials. From Sophia: "As the Psalms of David inspire many generations, I pray this volume will inspire today's saints! Be blessed!"

P.O. Box 453
Powder Springs, Georgia 30127
770.727.6517

info@entegritypublishing.com
www.entegritypublishing.com

CPSIA information can be obtained
at www.ICGtesting.com
Printed in the USA
LVHW05s0415020918
588728LV00004B/6/P